This is the story of 101 Dalmatians.
You can read along with me in your
book. You will know it is time to turn
the page when you hear the chimes
ring like this...

Let's begin now.

Pongo (Narrator)	Michael Gough
Roger	Jeff Bennett
Anita	Mary Kay Bergman
Horace	Brian Cummings
Jasper	Barry Dennen
Mr Tibbs	Richard Endman
Perdita	Linda Gary
Cruella De Vil	Betty Lou Gerson
Puppy	Bradley Pierce
Nanny	Russi Taylor
Colonel	Hal Smith

Produced by Ted Kryczko and Randy Thornton
Music from the Walt Disney Records Music Library, Jim Andron and
Gary Powell composers

Dalmatian Plantation
Performed by Chorus
Music and Lyrics by Mel Leven
© 1959 Walt Disney Music Company (ASCAP). © renewed. All rights
reserved. International © secured.
℗ 1996 Walt Disney Records

Cruella De Vil
Performed by Bill Lee, Lisa Davis and Ben Wright
Music and Lyrics by Mel Leven
© 1959 Walt Disney Music Company (ASCAP). © renewed. All rights
reserved. International © secured.
℗ 1996 Walt Disney Records

First edition published by Parragon in 2010

Parragon
Queen Street House
4 Queen Street
Bath BA1 1HE, UK

℗ 2010 Walt Disney Records © Disney
Copyright © 2010 Disney Enterprises, Inc.
Based on the book The Hundred and One Dalmatians by Dodie
Smith, published by William Heinemann Ltd.

ISBN: 978-1-4454-4156-6

Printed in China

Hello. My name is Pongo, and I'm a Dalmatian. That's a stylish dog with spots. I live in London with my master, Roger. He's a clever fellow who writes songs all day long. That gets rather dull after a while, but at least we take a walk in the park every day.

It was in the park, in fact, that I spotted my perfect mate – Perdita, a beautiful lady Dalmatian. Her owner was a lovely young woman named Anita. But Roger didn't even notice her.

I couldn't let this chance go by. Pulling at my leash, I raced in front of Anita!

'Pongo! Where are you ... ooof! Oh, I beg your pardon, Miss.'

And so you could say that I brought Roger and Anita together.

Soon, they were husband and wife. Perdita and I couldn't have been happier.

After that, life was far from dull. Our first chore was to turn Roger's messy bachelor flat into a real household. It was no easy task! I suppose that's why we hired Nanny, our cook and housekeeper. Soon, the place was the perfect home for two couples just starting out.

Life was grand. And one day, Perdita gave me wonderful news. 'Pongo, dear, we're expecting puppies!'

Finally, the big day arrived. Nanny was so excited! 'Mister, Missus! The little ones are here.'

We rushed into the kitchen. There sat my proud Perdita, with fifteen adorable puppies.

Roger and I danced around the room. 'Pongo, old boy! Congratulations!'

Then, a harsh knocking cut our celebration short. Nanny opened the door, and there stood Anita's old classmate, Cruella De Vil!

Perdita trembled. 'Oh, Pongo! It's that evil woman.'

Cruella swept into the kitchen, wrapped in expensive furs. 'Anita, darling! I heard you were expecting Dalmatian puppies. I'll buy every single one of them.'

But then Cruella caught sight of our puppies. 'Ugh!
They're mongrels, Anita. No spots!'

'No, Cruella. Dalmatians are born white. They'll get their
spots in a few weeks.'

'Oh! Then I'll take them all!'

Roger saw Perdita's frightened look. 'No! We're not selling the puppies. *You* won't get a single one!'

Cruella sneered. 'All right! Keep the little beasts! But you'll be sorry!'

The next few weeks passed quickly. The puppies all grew and got their spots. Nanny watched over them like a proud grandmother.

Each puppy was different from the others. Rolly was always hungry. Lucky got into mischief. Penny and Patch were never apart. But they all loved to watch television.

Their favourite programme was *Thunderbolt, the Wonder Dog*. Each week, the pups cheered as their hero brought another criminal to justice.

One winter evening, Anita, Roger, Perdita and I went for a walk in the park. The puppies were left at home, under the watchful eye of Nanny. While we were gone, two suspicious-looking men knocked at the door.

'Excuse me, Madame. We are here to read the electric metre.'

'Oh, no you're not! No! You can't come in here!'

But the two pushed their way into the house, locked Nanny in the attic, and stole all the puppies!

No-one, not even the police, could solve the case. Perdy and I were beside ourselves with grief.

'I'm afraid it's up to us now. We'll use the twilight bark to alert all the dogs in London and in the villages nearby .'

My message passed from dog to dog, over the city and through the towns.

It was late at night when the call reached the village of Suffolk.

An old sheepdog woke up. 'Hmmm ... I say, it's an alert! One long howl, two short, one yip and a woof. Fifteen little Dalmatians have disappeared?'

Sergeant Tibs, the cat, sprang to attention. 'Colonel, sir! Two nights past, I heard puppies barking at the old De Vil mansion.'

'Well, then, you'd better do some scouting. On the double, Tibs!' 'Right-o, sir!'

Sergeant Tibs approached the crumbling mansion. Cautiously, he peeked through a dusty window. 'I was right! Dalmatian puppies! But there are more here than fifteen!'

Actually, there were ninety-nine puppies, plus the two crooks, Horace and Jasper, and one Cruella De Vil!

'Finish it tonight! I don't care how you get rid of them! I want my spotted coat by morning, do you hear?'

Sergeant Tibs raced back to report to the Colonel, who sped the message to us, in London.

'Perdy, they have found the puppies at the old De Vil mansion, in Suffolk!'

'But it's so far, Pongo, and it's beginning to snow. We must leave right now!'

Meanwhile, Sergeant Tibs returned to the De Vil mansion. Luckily, Horace and Jasper were too busy watching television to notice.

'Pssst, puppies! Come with me if you want to save your skins!'

One by one, the puppies crept through a hole in the wall.

Tibs was boosting the last pups out when the crooks spotted them. 'They're getting away, Horace!'

At that moment, Perdita and I burst into the house.

Snarling and snapping, we kept Horace and Jasper busy, while the pups escaped into the night.

We all headed for the Colonel's old barn, where Perdy stared at the dozens of extra puppies. 'Why would Cruella want so many, Sergeant Tibs?'

'She was going to make coats out of them, Ma'am.'

'She's a devil. A witch! Oh, Pongo, what'll we do?'

'We have to get all the puppies back to London somehow.'

Tibs cocked an ear. 'Colonel, sir, there's a truck heading this way. Horace and Jasper are following our tracks!'

'We'll hold them off to the bitter end, Sergeant. Pongo, you'd better head out the back way.'

Horace and Jasper stepped right into the Colonel's trap. As the old sheepdog kept them at bay, Captain the horse took aim and kicked both the crooks right through the barn wall!

Horace and Jasper limped back to the mansion, where they found Cruella waiting for them.

'You fools! Get in the truck and find those puppies!'

Meanwhile, we struggled across the snowy countryside, looking for shelter. A friendly cocker spaniel put us up in a warm dairy barn, but we weren't safe yet. We heard the crooks' truck driving by.

Perdita was worried. 'They're looking for us, Pongo. I don't know how we're going to slip past them.'

Happily fed, the
puppies began to play
in a pile of coal.

Perdita gasped.
'Why, Pongo. They're
all black!'

'Perdy, what a
great idea! We'll all
roll in the dust and
disguise ourselves.
Cruella won't
recognize us!'

Meanwhile, the
cocker spaniel
found us a ride
home to London,
in a moving van. Perdy
and I were loading the puppies
into the van when Cruella drove by.
Unfortunately, a drop of snow fell
onto my coat and washed away the
soot.

Cruella saw me, and slammed on
the brakes. 'It's the Dalmatians!'

I tossed the last puppy into the van, just as Cruella raced after us.

'You little beasts! You can't get away this time!' Ranting and raving, she lost control of her car and crashed!

Cruella crawled out of the wreck. 'My coat! My beautiful spotted coat! It's gone forever!'

We were safe at last, and on our way back to London.

That evening, Roger heard a scratch at the door.
'Anita! Come here! The puppies are back!'

'Oh, Roger, how wonderful!
But there are so many! What will
we do with them all?'
    'We'll keep them!'

Roger was so happy, he sat down at his piano to compose a song. 'Let's see, ninety-nine puppies ... add Pongo and Perdita, and that makes 101 Dalmatians! Just think, Anita, we'll buy a big place in the country and start ... a Dalmatian plantation!'

And that's exactly what we did.

The End